I dedicate this book to my wife's grandmother, Alberta Vickerman. She certainly had a great memory when it came to remembering the time I got *Burger King* on the way to her Thanksgiving dinner!

ɹʇ Press

Boys Town, Nebraska

How Do I Remember All That?

A Story to Improve Working Memory

Written by
Bryan Smith

Illustrated by
Lisa M. Griffin

How Do I Remember All That

Text and Illustrations Copyright © 2021 by Father Flanagan's Boys' Home
ISBN: 978-1-944882-72-3

Published by the Boys Town Press
13603 Flanagan Blvd.
Boys Town, NE 68010

For a Boys Town Press catalog, call **1-800-282-6657**
or visit our website: **BoysTownPress.org**

Publisher's Cataloging-in-Publication Data

Names: Smith, Bryan (Bryan Kyle), 1978- author. | Griffin, Lisa M., 1972- illustrator.

Title: How do I remember all that? : a story to improve working memory / written by Bryan Smith ; illustrated by Lisa M. Griffin.

Description: Boys Town, NE : Boys Town Press, [2021] | Series: Executive FUNction. | Audience: grades K-5. | Summary: As his schoolwork gets tougher, Braden becomes more frustrated. In this humorous story, Braden learns strategies to breakdown complex problems into smaller, manageable tasks and is shown practical tools for improving his memory.--Publisher.

Identifiers: ISBN: 978-1-944882-72-3

Subjects: LCSH: Memory in children--Juvenile fiction. | Short-term memory in children--Juvenile fiction. | Learning disabilities--Treatment--Juvenile fiction. | Stress management for children--Juvenile fiction. | Planning in children--Juvenile fiction. | Learning, Psychology of--Juvenile fiction. | Self-reliance in children--Juvenile fiction. | Children--Life skills guides--Juvenile fiction. | CYAC: Memory--Fiction. | Learning disabilities--Fiction. | Stress management--Fiction. | Planning--Fiction. | Learning--Psychology--Fiction. | Self-reliance-- Fiction. | Conduct of life--Fiction. | BISAC: JUVENILE FICTION / Social Themes / Self- Esteem & Self-Reliance. | JUVENILE FICTION / Disabilities & Special Needs. | EDUCATION / Special Education / Learning Disabilities. | SELF-HELP / Personal Growth / Memory Improvement. | JUVENILE NONFICTION / Social topics / Self-Esteem & Self-Reliance.

Classification: LCC: PZ7.1.S597 H69 2021 | DDC: [Fic]--dc23

Printed in the United States
10 9 8 7 6 5 4 3 2 1

Boys Town Press is the publishing division of Boys Town,
a national organization serving children and families.

Hey everyone, Braden here.

Does anyone else feel like school gets harder every year? Pretty soon it is going to be **impossible.**

3

I remember when reading just meant you read a few sentences and maybe answered one question. Now, we read long stories and need to remember everything about it! This happened just the other day.

My teacher, Mrs. Brookshire, passed out a reading story that was **about a thousand pages long!** I was so happy once I finished it, but then I read the first question.

"1. How did Tim feel when he went to the park?"
I groaned loudly.

Mrs. Brookshire could tell I was having a hard time. She walked over and asked me what was wrong? I told her, "This story is about a kid named Louis. Who is Tim, and why do I need to know how he felt?"

6

Mrs. Brookshire talked to me about the details of the story and how they're important indicators. I told her...

Mrs. Brookshire talked to me about how breaking down assignments into smaller, more manageable tasks can help with something called "working memory."

She asked if I knew my phone number? I responded, **"Sure, that's easy. Why did you ask me that?"**

"That's because phone numbers are broken down into three sets of numbers," she said.

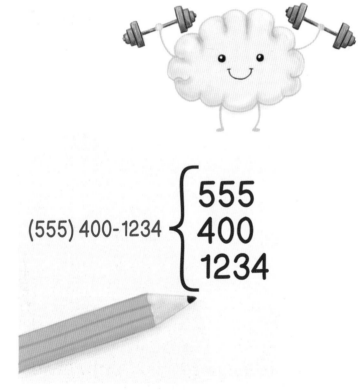

(555) 400-1234
555
400
1234

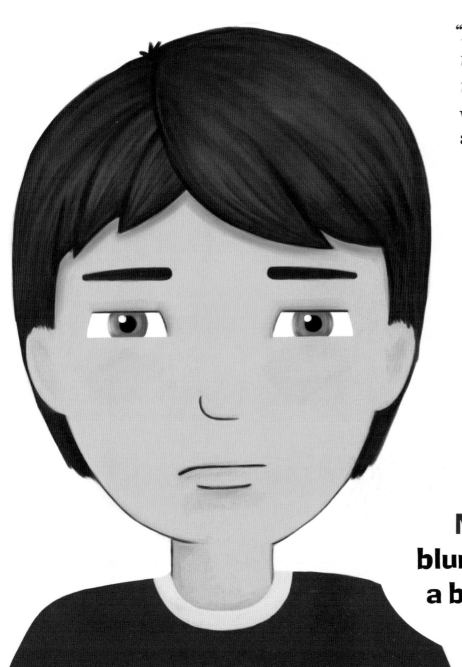

"It's easier to remember things when you break them down. Now, tell me what you see when you look at this story?"

NOTHING. It all blurs together and is a big jumbled mess.

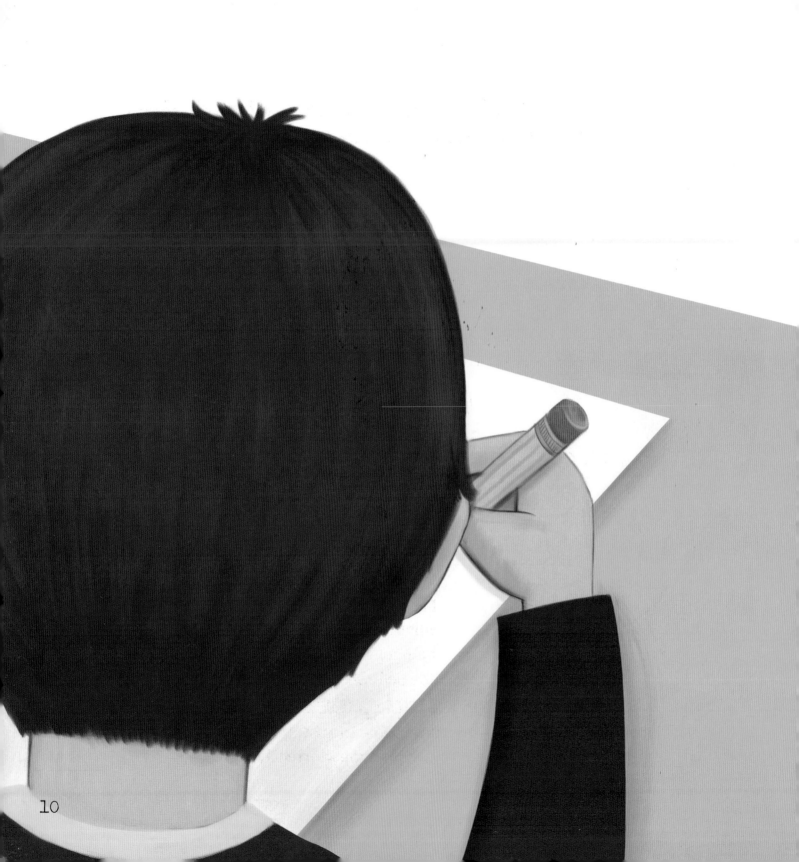

Mrs. Brookshire replied, *"That's my point. We need to break it down. Let's cover up everything but the first paragraph."*

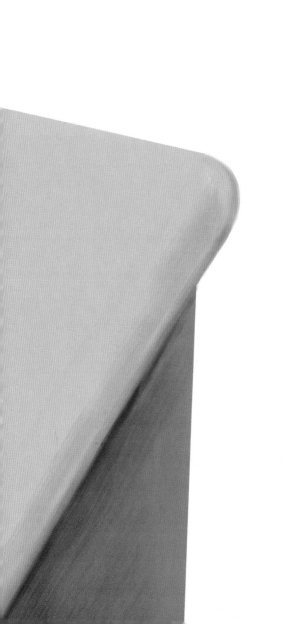

She taught me the
"STOP AND JOT"
method to help me remember
in situations like this.

This is where after each passage,
I write a short sentence about
what the paragraph was about to
help remember everything. Things
seemed a lot clearer after that.
And guess what?
I was able to answer most of
the questions correctly.

Mrs. Brookshire told me how proud she was of me and reminded me the next time I get stuck to ask for help following our classroom rules.

STOP AND JOT WORKSHEET

PARAGRAPH	SUMMARY
3	This story is about a kid named Louis who lost his dog. His brother, Tim, helped him find Fluffy.
5	Louis was so sad and was worried that Fluffy was hungry and scared.
9	Louis and Tim found Fluffy down in the basement asleep in the laundry basket. They were so relieved.

It wasn't long before I found out this wasn't just a school problem. I had just checked off my list of what I had to do for homework and sat down for dinner. After we were done, Mom told me to clean the dishes, finish my reading, and get my backpack ready for school the next day.

Just as I got to the sink, my mind went blank on what all Mom told me to do. I just kept thinking about my homework. I walked over to Mom and said, **"There's a lot. How do I remember all that stuff you told me to do?"**

"Well, besides making a list, another tip is to make a connection," she said.

"A what?"

"A *connection*," she said again. "Have I ever told you how I remembered the order of the planets from the sun?" Mom asked.

"No," I replied.

15

"My Very Excellent Mother Just Served Us Nachos," she said.

"What? How does eating nachos have anything to do with planets?" I asked.

16

Mom explained how she took the first letter in each planet and made a funny saying to help her remember the order.

*"**MY** starts with **M**. This helps me remember Mercury is the first planet closest to the sun."*

Oh cool!

Mom reminded me of the things I needed to get done and said I should try and create my own way to help me remember those things.

I thought for a minute and then said,
"Clean my book in my backpack."
Mom looked confused.

"Do what?" she said.

"I came up with a way of remembering what needs to get done.

Clean reminds me to clean the dishes,

book reminds me to read my book, and

backpack reminds me to get my backpack ready."

In no time I was done with all three things. **Maybe my memory was finally working.**

Well, that is until I got to math class that Friday. I was working on some word problems. I had no idea what operation to use, so I just started writing 'no clue' beside each problem. Mrs. Brookshire could see I was frustrated and asked, "Braden, how are things going?"

I explained I was frustrated, but how the stop and jot idea didn't work in math. Mrs. Brookshire agreed. She talked to me about visualizing the problem. ***"Take a look at this problem,"*** she said. ***"I want you to visualize what is going on."***

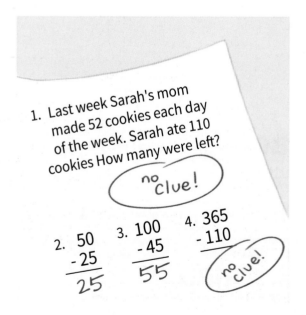

1. Last week Sarah's mom made 52 cookies each day of the week. Sarah ate 110 cookies How many were left?

no Clue!

2. 50
   - 25
   ———
   25

3. 100
   - 45
   ———
   55

4. 365
   - 110
   ———
   no Clue!

She read, *"Sarah's mom made* **52 cookies** *every day of the week. How do we figure out how many cookies she made?"*

"That's easy. It's 52x7 so that's... um... 364 cookies." I laughed and said, **"That's a ton of cookies."**

"I know, but can you see it?" she asked.

"Yes," I said.

"Ok, great. Now it says *Sarah ate* *110 cookies,"* she said.

Whoa, that has to be a record!

Mrs. Brookshire smiled. "Now, read the last sentence."

I read, **"How many cookies were left?"**

Mrs. Brookshire asked, "Does it make more sense to add or subtract to find the total?"

"Well, since she basically stole the cookies and left everyone else with less, it has to be subtract," I said.

"Great. Now keep visualizing the word problems to help with your working memory," she said.

As I continued reading, I kept laughing at some of the problems because they were pretty funny when I visualized them. It wasn't long before I was done.

I was shocked when I got them all right!

Guess I might be trying this more often to help with my working memory.

That weekend, my little cousin Matt was coming over so my uncle and aunt could go to a wedding. My aunt asked if Blake and I could help Matt with his homework.

How hard could that be with a kid in pre-school? **You won't believe how easy his homework was.**

All he had to do was memorize the days of the week. I heard Blake having him say the days over and over, but that wasn't working.

And that's when I remembered how I learned the days of the week.

Singing to the tune of the Addam's family song, **I came in singing...**

Days of the week *(snap, snap)…*
Days of the week *(snap, snap)…*
Days of the week, days of the week, days of the week *(snap, snap)…*
There's Sunday and there's Monday.

There's Tuesday and there's Wednesday.

There's Thursday and there's Friday.

And then there's Saturday.

Days of the week *(snap, snap)…*
Days of the week *(snap, snap)…*
Days of the week, days of the week, days of the week *(snap, snap)…*

30

TIPS

for **Parents** and **Educators**

Working memory is a valuable skill for children to master.

This can help them be successful in school and later in life as an adult. Some children (and adults) seem to excel in this area, and others have more challenges. Use the following tips to help practice and improve working memory.

1. Have your child teach you a new skill or concept. Make sure to tell her to say the steps in order and give as many details as possible. If she leaves out a step, follow it just as she told you in order to demonstrate the importance of details and order.

2. Have your child create a picture in his head of something he just read or learned. Ask him to describe in detail what he is picturing.

3. Play memory games like Uno® or Go Fish. Children have to remember the rules of the game AND cards they have seen or that other people have.

4. To help children not get overwhelmed, break longer assignments into smaller more manageable tasks. Having children repeat directions back to you sometimes also helps.

5. Help your children stay organized by organizing homework, their rooms, or their schedules. Creating routines at home and school helps children stay on track.

6. Make sure to praise your child even for little things she remembers to do.

7. Allow children breaks to help reset their brains. Examples might be going for a walk, drawing, or playing with playdough.

8. Use a multisensory approach to learning new material. You can do this by using visuals, singing songs, and doing some movement activities. For example, to help your children learn their ABCs, you could have him sing them, match them, and write them in shaving cream with his finger.

BOYS TOWN®
Saving Children   Healing Families

For more parenting information, visit boystown.org/parenting.

Boys Town Press books by Bryan Smith

Executive FUNction

Stories that teach children how to plan, organize, manage time and maintain self-control!

978-1-944882-50-1

978-1-944882-45-7

978-1-944882-60-0

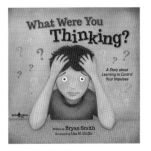

978-1-934490-96-9

OTHER TITLE: My Day Is Ruined!

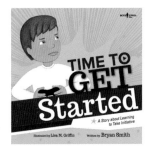

978-1-944882-31-0

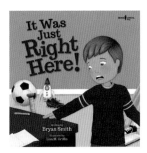

978-1-944882-20-4

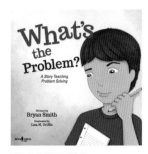

978-1-944882-38-9

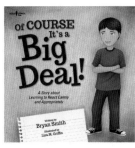

978-1-944882-11-2

Downloadable Activities
Go to BoysTownPress.org to download.

WITHOUT LIMITS
dream • connect • soar

Young readers learn how to be more giving, more understanding and more resilient!

Everyone's Contributions Count
Stress Stinks
Diversity is Key
Mindset Matters
Kindness Counts
Empathy is My Superpower!

Other Titles

But I Need Your Help Now!

When I Couldn't Get Over It, I Learned to Start Acting Differently

Is There an App for That?

If Winning Isn't Everything, Why Do I Hate to Lose?

BOYS TOWN® Press

BoysTownPress.org

For information on Boys Town, its Education Model®, Common Sense Parenting®, and training programs:
boystowntraining.org | boystown.org/parenting
training@BoysTown.org | 1-800-545-5771

For parenting and educational books and other resources:
BoysTownPress.org
btpress@BoysTown.org | 1-800-282-6657